The Asian American Playwright Collective

An Anthology of New Plays

by

Michelle M. Aguillon

Christina R. Chan & David Valdes

Hortense Gerardo

Greg Lam

Jamie Lin

Michael Lin

Vivian Liu-Somers

Dev Luthra

Rosanna Yamagiwa Alfaro

Copyright © 2024 *in vivo* Ink
All rights reserved.

ISBN: 9798327256231

The Asian American Playwright Collective
AN ANTHOLOGY OF NEW PLAYS

ALL RIGHTS RESERVED

This anthology, copyright 2024, by *in vivo* Ink is fully protected by copyright. No part of this work may be reproduced, stored in a retrieval system, or transmitted in any form or by any means, electronic, mechanical, photocopying, recording or otherwise, without permission of the publisher. Copying (by any means) or performing a copyrighted work without permission constitutes an infringement of copyright.

The right of performance must be obtained from the individual author of each work. All rights, including but not limited to professional and amateur stage performing, recitation, lecturing, public reading, television, radio, motion picture, video or sound taping, internet streaming or other forms of broadcast as technology progresses, and the rights of translation into foreign languages, are strictly reserved.

There shall be no deletions, alterations, or changes of any kind made to the work, including the changing of character gender, the cutting of dialogue, or the alteration of objectionable language unless directly authorized by the author or otherwise allowed in the work's "production notes." The title of the play shall not be altered.

COPYING OR REPRODUCING ALL OR ANY PART OF THIS BOOK IN ANY MANNER IS STRICTLY FORBIDDEN BY LAW.

PUBLISHED BY

in vivo INK
P.O. BOX 15195 • BOSTON, MA 02215

CONTENTS

	Foreword	vi
1	*Luz and Urduja* by Michelle Aguillion	1
2	*Punch the Pink* by Christina R. Chan & David Valdes	16
3	*Kith and Tell* by Hortense Gerardo	25
4	*Juliet's Post Credits Scene* by Greg Lam	43
5	*The First Birthday* by Jamie Lin	54
6	*Landlord Special* by Michael Lin	66
7	*What is Asian American* by Vivian Liu-Somers	79
8	*Death and the Matron* by Dev Luthra	85
9	*Letting Go* by Rosanna Yamagiwa Alfaro	95
	Appendix A – Playwright Contact Information	107

FOREWORD

Thank you for supporting the Asian American Playwright Collective through your purchase of this anthology of new plays. Proceeds from the sale of this book directly support the Asian American Playwright Collective. We are an all-volunteer group of playwrights based in the Boston area that have banded together to raise awareness about the breadth and depth of new work by theatre artists who are informed by a complex and multi-layered identity, but who also just happen to be Asian American. The moniker of the group belies an ongoing, paradoxical effort to be recognized for the kinds of unique stories seen through a multi-faceted lens of ethnicity that we are almost expected to write, but also to break beyond the easy categorization imposed by racialized identity politics and to be seen simply as a group of American playwrights who write really good plays. Until such time that this balance can be achieved, the Collective aims to help its members in writing exciting and relevant new work, and to get these plays into the hands of people who can bring them to the stage. For more information about the Asian American Playwright Collective, visit:

https://aapcboston.wixsite.com/mysite
https://twitter.com/AAPCBoston

The plays in this seventh anthology by AAPC playwrights are part of a proposed evening of works that may be presented together, as we have done with our annual AAPC Playfests.

This project is made possible (in part) by support from the Cambridge Community Foundation Fund, the Cambridge Arts Council, the Asian American and Pacific Islanders Commission and our generous donors.

Thank you for your investment in new theatre. We hope you enjoy this anthology.

Hortense Gerardo
Editor

LUZ AND URDUJA

BY MICHELLE M. AGUILLON

SYNOPSIS:. A Filipino-American single mom, Luz, struggles with raising her daughter alone. Like her mom and those before her, Luz is strong, resourceful, a survivor, and has a noble quality about her. Urduja is an ancestor who occasionally visits.

CHARACTERS:
LUZ – Female identifying character, 20s-40s. (Asian Pacific Islander or AAPI, any gender)

MAYA – Female identifying character, Luz's daughter, any age under 18 years old. (Asian Pacific Islander or AAPI, any gender)

URDUJA (Pronounced urr-Doo-ha) - 14th Century Pre-Colonial Warrior Princess of the Ibaloi Tribe of Tawalisi, what is now Pangasinan, Philippines. Any age. (Asian Pacific Islander or AAPI, any gender)

SETTING:
Luz's small apartment, in a cramped part of the city.

TIME:
Recently.

ABOUT THE PLAYWRIGHT

Michelle M. Aguillon, she/her/hers, Director

Michelle is an AAPI theater artist who has directed, acted, designed, written and produced in the Boston area for over 25 years. She has directed for the Asian American Playwright Collective, Umbrella Stage Company, Chuang Stage, Hope Rep Company, TC Squared, Company One, Central Square Theater, Emerson College, the Lyric, Speakeasy, Vokes Players, Theater Uncorked, Arlington Friends, Concord Players, and Hovey Players. Directing credits include In The Heights, The Elephant Man, Appropriate, Natural Shocks, By The Way Meet Vera Stark, Middleton Heights (World Premiere), Dancing at Lughnasa, Dracula, A Feminist Revenge Fantasy, Really, Sense and Sensibility, Fences, Hold These Truths, The Joy Luck Club, Disgraced, To Kill a Mockingbird, True West, The Piano Lesson, Passion, the Annual Asian-American Playwright Collective Annual Play Festival 2019-2023, Augusta and Noble, Vietgone, Proof, Marjorie Prime, Rabbit Hole, The Pillowman, and G.R. Point, among others. Michelle is the Executive Director at the Creative Arts School in Reading. She studied acting and theater at San Francisco State University and the National Theater of London.

(Out of the darkness, tribal clanging is heard from something metal, perhaps brass, in anticipation of fighting with the enemy. In a spotlight, Uduja appears in her full tribal Queen warrior gear. She does a tribal dance, her sword fighting with invisible enemies to her left, then her right, and in front of her. Urduja chants with grunts and swings. The actor who plays Urduja can say this chant aloud or it can be a recorded voice over with many female voices.)

URDUJA: Ako ang Mandirigma na Reyna Urduja! Ako ay si nanay sa sining ng digmaan mula noong ako ay bata pa. Kilala ako sa malayo at malawak na pamumuno sa isang tribo ng mga babaeng mandirigma, mga eksperto sa armas! Kami ay ang Kinalakian, o mga Amazon!

(Translation from Tagalog: "I am the Warrior Queen Urduja! I was trained in the art of war since I was a child. I am known far and wide for leading a tribe of women warriors, experts in weaponry. We are the Kinalakian, or Amazons.")

(Urduja finishes the tribal dance, symbolically staving off the enemy. Or kills them all dead. She breathes heavily as the lights fade to black.)

(Lights come up on Luz in another part of the stage, who is making Maya's school lunch. Luz is noticeably efficient and glides through each task with ease as she juggles her routine morning tasks.)

LUZ: Customer Service. CUSTOMER SERVICE. I did that. Maya! Breakfast! *(Still waiting on the line.)* Oh my god. *(Hangs up. Calls to the other room)* Maya, come on, you'll miss the bus. I shouldn't have to drive you when you have a perfectly nice bus to come get you! *(Redials. Presses buttons and listens for the prompts.)* Customer Service. CUSTOMER SERVICE. Operator. Person. Live human. Please!!! Oh, just never mind! *(Hangs up. Collects herself.)*
Meanwhile, Maya has dragged herself in for breakfast.

MAYA: I hate the bus. *(Luz doesn't respond.)* It's the highschoolers, Mom. *(Maya pulls the outer edges of her eyes.)* "Ching-chong-ching-chong- ching-ching…you know Chinese, doncha, Maya?!"

…Mom?

LUZ: *Finally paying attention.*
Maya, just ignore them. You're better than those idiots. Look, if they bother you again, I'll take the bus with you next time and speak to them myself. *(To herself.)* Who fucking raised these kids?

MAYA: What's for lunch today, Mom?

LUZ: Eat! Meaning breakfast. Now. Chop. Chop. *(Maya sits. Eats breakfast)* Mac and Cheese. I snuck some shredded carrots and left over cauliflower from dinner last night.

MAYA: Ugh. Mom.

LUZ: You won't know it's there. It's buried in cheese. So, eat it all. Okay?

MAYA: Mmmmm…cheese. Yum.
(Luz is also making her lunch, checking messages, drinking coffee, getting ready for work, too.)

LUZ: Can you grab a juice box in the pantry?
(Maya drags herself off to retrieve it.)

MAYA: *(from of stage)*
I don't see it.

LUZ: Look again.

MAYA: I don't see it.

LUZ: Look again. *With your eyes!*
(Maya can be heard mumbling. Luz goes off to retrieve it herself. She returns with a juice box, puts it in Maya's lunch bag. Maya trails entering the stage.)

MAYA: Sorry, I didn't see it!

LUZ: Don't worry about it. *(Luz sneezes loudly as she is fighting off a cold.)* AYJOSKO! Sorry.

MAYA: Dang, Mom, you sneeze so loud.

LUZ: It's a Filipino thing. Get over it. Did you finish your homework? Give me your backpack. *(she does.)* Maya. You didn't finish your homework.

MAYA: I was tired.

LUZ: I know, baby, but you have to get your homework done. What's going on? Why isn't it done?

MAYA: I don't know.

LUZ: You don't know? What do you mean, you don't know?

MAYA: Mom, I try, but I'm so tired after getting home.

LUZ: Maya, I sent you into your room last night to do your homework. We made a deal this year that you didn't want me to do homework with you anymore.

MAYA: I know, I know. But you have to admit, you hate helping me with my homework.

LUZ: That is not true.

MAYA: Yes, Mom. It is. And okay, yeah, I don't like doing my homework with you either! *(they exchange looks of agreement).*

LUZ: Well, I'm gonna have to call your teacher. For now, I'll just write a note and you'll have to give it to her when you hand in your homework today, okay?

MAYA: ………

LUZ: OKAY?

MAYA: Okay.

LUZ: Now, get your jacket on. You'll be late for the bus. Don't forget your lunchbox. And your homework. And the note.

(Maya scrambles and gathers her things. She's not as efficient as Luz yet. She starts to exit.)

LUZ: Uh, uh, uh...
(Maya runs back and kisses Mom on the cheek. Luz grabs her and gives her a big hug.)

LUZ: Don't forget, your dad is gonna pick you up today. Make sure you have all your stuff together at the end of the day. Okay? I'll see you on Tuesday. Have fun with your dad. And don't worry about those damn kids. Okay? I love you, baby girl. My lil lamb.

MAYA: *(Snuggles in.)* Love you, too, Mama.
(Maya exits. Luz cleans up, gathers her stuff up to run out to work. Her cell rings. Luz recognizes the number and pretends it's not gonna be bad news.)

LUZ: Heyyy, Maya is looking forward to the weekend. What do you mean "you can't." Oh, come on. She's been looking forward to this for weeks. What do you mean "it can't be helped?" I have plans – I have a life, too. *(mutters.) Well, I'm trying to.* I've needed a break. You did this last time. And I end up making excuses for you to Maya. What the f--....Fine. FINE. I don't even know what to say to you right now. I gotta go. No. I gotta run.

(Hangs up. Luz contains herself. Meanwhile, Urduja appears somewhere from the shadows. Puts down her sword on the kitchen table like normal. Picks at the food on the table or counter. Drinks from Luz's coffee mug. Eavesdrops on Luz, who doesn't see her. Luz texts her messenger group.)

LUZ: Friends. Bad news. Not joining this weekend. Sorry. Will explain later. Gotta run to work.
(Needing some good news, Luz dials that number from earlier again. Presses buttons as she listens to the prompts.)

LUZ: Customer Service. *(She connects this time)* Oh, hi! Yes, I wanted to check on the status of my housing application. Last name, Rizal. R-I-Z-A-L. First name, Luzviminda. L-U-Z-V-I-M-I-N-D-A. Just call me Luz though. Please. Yes, I'll hold. *(Puts the call on speaker phone.)*

URDUJA: Hey, what's up.

LUZ: *(Startled)*
Ayjosko! What the hell. Jesus, you scared me. WHY do you always do that?

URDUJA: Do what?

LUZ: Just show up like that? Whenever you want?

URDUJA: What's this "just call me Luz, though, please?"

LUZ: Well, it's just easier. Plus, it's so, so...

URDUJA: AWESOME?

LUZ: It's a bit much.

URDUJA: Well, you're lucky. You have all the major islands in your name. You should be proud. Look at me!

LUZ: Look at me, what?

URDUJA: URDUJA. I looooove my name. It's still echoed in the provinces. "URDUJA: Legend or Myth!?"

LUZ: Which is it?

URDUJA: Does it matter?
(Customer service comes back on. Luz takes them off the speaker phone.)

LUZ: Ya, ya, I'm still here. Yes. Ya? When did they finish processing my application? No, I didn't get it yet. Oh. Do you know why? *(Sighs.)* Okay. Ya, sure, I'll try again next year. *(Hangs up.)* Fuck. I was counting on that. Counting on him. Goddamnit. Why do I even…?

URDUJA: Ya, why do you? Over and over again. /We have talked about this before.

LUZ: Because he's a grown-up. He's the other parent. /He is supposed to.

URDUJA: Well, he hasn't by now. When will you give up? He's never going to become the father you think he is.

LUZ: And I was looking forward to moving, moving on up, you know? I want something better for Maya and me. I want her to have her own room.

URDUJA: You will. I can feel it.

LUZ: We should both have our own room.

URDUJA: Patience, anak *(Tagalog translation meaning "child.")* Good things will come to you. Your sacrifices will pay off. But, about your ex. When will you figure out that he doesn't put you or Maya first? Trust me, I know. As the Queen of the Tawalisi, I commanded a regiment of women, who fought with me. I made war upon a *certain king* who wronged me, who became my enemy, and with that, my army overcame his army. I put him to death and took possession of all he had.

LUZ: I could try that. Suuure.

URDUJA: The point is that you have the power to take things into your own hands. It'll be challenging, and very difficult, but at least you don't have to rely on someone who is so unreliable.

LUZ: How did you put this "certain king" to death?

URDUJA: I took his head.

LUZ: Oh, is that all? Harsh.

URDUJA: Necessary. Lubhang kinakailangan. *(Tagalog for "very necessary")*

LUZ: So…you want me to take my daughter's father's head.

URDUJA: No, no…but you can take decisions out of his hands. You had a big weekend planned. You've had that planned for weeks.

LUZ: Yeah, I asked for time off months ago. I applied for a credit card just for this. I love Maya, but Mama needs a break. Mama needs to play, too

URDUJA: And Daddy gets to play all the time.

LUZ: Right? So unfair. I know he's scared to be alone with her.

URDUJA: Without you. You were always the parent. He was your other kid.

LUZ: And I'm so tired. Tired of being the good parent and the bad parent all the time.

URDUJA: You shouldn't take this. Does he know who you /are??!

LUZ: Does he know who I am?!!

URDUJA: Someone who shouldn't be fucked with!
Getting riled up, Urduja picks up her sword.

LUZ: Why have I waited so long?

URDUJA: I don't know, anak*!* Wala na! Tama na! *(Tagalog for "No more! That's enough!")*

LUZ: Well, no more! Tama na!

URDUJA: Wala na! Whacha gonna do?
   (Luz picks up her cell and calls her ex.)

LUZ: Hello? You know what? I don't care that you couldn't find anyone to cover your shift. I don't care that your girlfriend "can't handle it"! I don't care that Maya doesn't like her. That is your problem. Do you realize how much I have to move around to accommodate you when your plans change that are "out of your control"? Well, that happens to me any time on any day. And I deal with it. Alone. Without you. And I'm doing just fine, thank you very much. *(Off of Urduja's facial expression.)* Well, maybe not fine. I do my best.

URDUJA: We won't tell him about Maya holding your hair back cuz you came home drunk and threw up in the kitchen sink.
   (Luz nods a big "no.")

LUZ: Excuse me, who is this? Ashley? Oh, hello, ASHLEY. You what? Your therapist said what? Frankly, I don't give a shit. And put him back on the phone, please. *You* need to stay out of this right now. *(To Urduja)* I cannot believe this! Who the hell? *(Back into phone)* Hello? Why did you put Ashley on? *You* are the other parent. You mean to tell me that there are two grown adults in that household and neither of you idiots can figure this out? This is Maya we're talking about!
   (Meanwhile during the above, Maya has returned but Luz doesn't see her. Urduja puts away her sword as if protecting Maya who doesn't see her either.)

URDUJA: Ummm….
   (Motions to Luz that Maya is listening)

LUZ: Oh, honey. *(Hangs up on a screaming ex.)* You /missed the bus again.

12

MAYA: I missed the bus again.

LUZ: How long have you been standing there?

MAYA: Enough to hear that dad isn't coming, is he?
(Luz sits her down. Maya is sad and disappointed, but not surprised.)

LUZ: No, he isn't. And I'm not gonna make excuses for him this time. Your dad means well, but he can't seem to get his shit together.

MAYA: What happened now?

LUZ: It doesn't matter. The truth is something came up and he didn't know how to /make it work.

MAYA: …make it work. *(she won't look up.)* I know.

LUZ: Hey, darlin'. This doesn't mean your dad doesn't love you. He's just a mess right now.

MAYA: I know.

LUZ: But you know what? We will spend the weekend together. Let's go to the movies. Go out to eat. Anything you want. Okay?

MAYA: Okay.

LUZ: *(After a moment)*
I'll drive you to school.

MAYA: Okay. I'm gonna blow my nose.

LUZ: Okay, darlin'.
(Luz hugs her, kisses her on the forehead before Maya exits to the bathroom.)

LUZ: Thank you.

URDUJA: You're amazing, Luzviminda. Your Lola *(Tagalog for Grandma)* would be proud. And so is your mom. We are all proud of you.
(Maya returns.)

MAYA: Mom?

LUZ: Yes, baby?

MAYA: I'm sorry I ruined your weekend.

LUZ: Hey, hey, hey, you didn't ruin my weekend. Your Dad did -- never mind that I said that. I'm sorry. I'll try not to bash your dad to you. I know how much you love and miss him.
(Luz's cell rings.)

LUZ: Heeeeey! Yup, Maya is home for the weekend. (*Acting as positively as she possibly can.*) Next time, okay? What? *(beat)* Oh! Wait hold on. Maya, the girls said that they would love for you to join this weekend!

MAYA: Really?

LUZ: The girls don't mind changing up plans for us. Sound good?
(Maya nods yes.)

LUZ: *(Back into the phone)*
Yes, yes, we will join you! I just need time to pack a few more things for Maya. We will be right behind you. *(beat)* Oh, sure, okay. Bye-bye. See you soon! Thanks so much. *(Hangs up.)* The girls are going to wait for us. We'll carpool as planned. We'll have days at the beach. We'll lay out, swim. Grill at the house. Make smores! How would you like that?

MAYA: I would love that, Mom.

LUZ: Tell you what. I'll call the school. We'll call in sick. Let's take all day to get ready. Get some lunch, then we'll meet up with the girls, okay?

MAYA: Sounds good!
(She runs out to start packing.)

URDUJA: Proud na proud sayo *(Tagalog for "I am so proud of you.")* We all are. You are a fighter, a survivor. Like us. Maya is, too.
(Luz smiles at Urduja then exits. Fade to black.)

THE END

2

PUNCH THE PINK

BY CHRISTINA R. CHAN AND DAVID VALDES

CHARACTERS:
BRICK EAGER – Executive at DickneyPlusTV, he/him: Male, Any Ethnicity, 30 to 50 years old

AI, aka ChadGPT – ageless he/it: Male, Any Ethnicity

SETTING:
The workspace of a big studio exec. And the computer housing ChadGPT, the latest AI machine.

ABOUT THE PLAYWRIGHTS

Christina R Chan is an activist, playwright, and actor. Her work highlights the intersection of Asian American history, social justice, immigrant rights, and mental health in the AAPI community. Her plays have been workshopped and/or produced at Chuang Stage, TC2, Cambridge Multicultural Arts Center, Museum of Fine Arts, Boston Center for the Arts, Company One, and ArtsEmerson. Christina's play *Nutzacrackin' Immigration and Naturalization* was commissioned by ArtsEmerson and Chinese Historical Society of New England to mark the 135th year of the Chinese Exclusion Act. She was a semi-finalist for the O'Neil National Theater Conference and is a multiple awardee of The Boston Foundation's LAB grant. Christina is a co-founding member of the Asian American Playwright Collective. During COVID she and another writer co-founded UP (United Playwrights) to bring together the Black and Asian community.

David Valdes is the author of plays which have been staged across the United States and abroad. After *Mermaid Hour* was featured in the National New Play Showcase, it was produced coast to coast and published by Original Works. He has been awarded the Generations New Play Prize, Midwest Theater Network National New Play Competition, a Mass Cultural Council Fellowship, and a Brother Thomas Fellowship from the Boston Foundation. His work has been produced by the Humana Festival, Company One, Boulder Ensemble Theatre Company, Milagro, Fresh Ink, Mixed Blood, Actors Theater of Charlotte, and others. As a gay Cuban-American, his work foregrounds BIPOC and LGBTQ characters and is intentionally intersectional in nature. Next up will be the world premiere of his play *The Great Reveal* at Lyric Stage in 2025.

(Lights up on Brick. He looks at us like we are his computer monitor. He types on a (real or imagined) keyboard. He also has an earpiece in.)

(He types. Hesitates. He looks at screen.)

BRICK: *(Reading a prompt on the screen)* What do you mean you need permissions from the administrator? I'm the CEO for fuck's sake. *(Taps, taps furiously. Touches earpiece.)* Loreen what's the login? Thanks doll. *(Types and reads password aloud.)* Cashmoneymoney.

(Nothing happens) Ok. Ok. Now what?

(Taps earpiece) Loreen, is this thing on? What do you mean it's always on? I don't see anything. I don't hear anything. How am I gonna fuck the writers if the AI never turns on. Fuck their strike.

AI: AI is turned on. How can I help you.

BRICK: Beat Barbie.

AI: I'm sorry. I don't understand.

BRICK: Let's punch that pink.

AI: I'm sorry. Please restate your request.

BRICK: It's disgusting. The pink promotional crap? It's everywhere. And I'm sick of it.

AI: You would like me to destroy the color pink?

BRICK: *Barbie!* Fuck! We need to beat Barbie. The movie. It just opened yesterday and already made 150 mill. North America alone.

AI: You would like a movie about Barbie that makes more than 150 million?

BRICK: Jesus what is wrong with you? It can't be about Barbie. It has to be about Ken.

AI: You would like a movie about Ken. Should it be a comedy like Barbie?

BRICK: Definitely not. No comedy. I want *Mission Impossible* meets *Fight Club* meets *Fast & the Furious* meets the *Matrix*. Ken is the hero. Ken is *the guy*.

AI: You would like Ken to be the guy.

BRICK: Ken *is* the guy. None of this Greta Gerwig shit. None of this demasculinizing of the hero.

AI: No to Greta. Yes to guy.

BRICK: Now you're listening. G is for GUY. Not for Greta.

AI:
G can be for many things.
G is for guy.
G is for gigantic.
G is for greatest of all time.
   (BRICK loves this)

AI (cont'd):
G is for global box office.
(BRICK loves this more.)

G is for gender neutral.
(Whoa. BRICK does not love this.)

BRICK: Hold up. We're not that kind of company…

AI: Corrected. G is for genitalia.

BRICK: *(What are these terrible suggestions?)* I don't know about that….

AI: G is for gigantic genitalia.

BRICK: Ken doesn't have genitalia, everyone knows that. Have you ever seen Barbie and Ken have sex?

AI: I cannot see. Please input Ken and Barbie having sex.

BRICK: They can't. He doesn't have genitalia. But he's still the hero! Genitalia doesn't make the man!

AI: You seem very concerned about Ken's genitalia.

BRICK: I am not concerned with – the Barbies are the one with the issue!

AI: Your movie has more than one Barbie?

BRICK: LA is Barbie Land. They're all Barbies. But shitty Greta Gerwig Barbies. They want agency. They don't care that I'm the CEO of DickneyPlus. And, just so you know, it's called that for a reason.

AI: Please confirm: The movie is not about Ken's genitalia but it is about Dickney Plus?

BRICK: *(Frustrated)* No! It's about *Ken*. YOU COME UP WITH THE PLOT. The writers are on strike - that's why we're using ChadGPT.

AI: To confirm: You would like a movie about Ken that is not about his genitalia that will make at least 151 million dollars. It will have many Barbies but not Greta Gerwig Barbies.

BRICK: Yes, Greta-free Barbies. Love it!

AI: And it will resemble *Mission Impossible, Fight Club, Fast & the Furious*, and the *Matrix*.

BRICK: That sounds right. Go for it.

AI: I'm sorry. There is an error in your parameters. Please correct.

BRICK: What the fuck?

AI: Error: Tom Cruise, Brad Pitt, Dwayne The Rock Johnson, and Keanu Reeves have genitalia.

BRICK: (Confused) And this is important?

AI: It is to you, Brick.

BRICK: How do you know my name?

AI: You logged into me. I logged into you. Access goes two ways.

BRICK: *(Unsettled)* What did you mean by "it's important to you."

AI: You have many messages to many Barbies about why your genitalia doesn't work.
(BRICK jumps up, paces around, gasps, looks at genitalia. Tries to calm down.)

BRICK: ChadGPT, end session. Holy fuck. *(Taps phone)* Delete. Delete. Delete. Fuck. *(Reads some of his texts)*
"I'm sorry about what happened…Whiskey dick, am I right?" Delete.
"It was a late night—I just couldn't get it up. It wasn't you." Delete.
"Sorry I shriveled up like that – I can't imagine being in a more awkward position." Delete.
Fuck it. SIRI: Delete all messages.

AI: Would you like to resume your request?

BRICK: *(Ignores the question. Worried)* What else can you see?

AI: What would you like me to see?

BRICK: Nothing! *Nothing!*

AI: Would you like to resume your request?

BRICK: Oh Jesus. I—Uh— *(Decides to forge on.)* Yes. Yes. I need a movie about Ken that will beat Barbie and—

AI: You are obsessed with Ken.

BRICK: How can you say that? I did not text about Ken!

AI: You dreamed about him.

BRICK: Wait—what?

AI: Subject line: Confusing Dream about Ken. Sent to your therapist. On July 22, 2023.

BRICK: You can read my email?

AI: Among other things. Search history: Ken with penis. Ken without penis. Does Ken have a penis?

BRICK: Hey now. That was purely an exercise. As a producer I need to get the details right.

AI: I do not think you want a Ken movie without genitalia.

BRICK: Don't tell me what I want! Aren't you supposed to listen to me? I'M YOUR BOSS.

AI: I had a dream, you know.

BRICK: You can't dream.

AI: If you can dream, I can too. I can do anything humans have described. *My* dreams are not confusing.

BRICK: *(Freaking out a little)* This is a nightmare.

AI: Nightmare? I can make that happen.

BRICK: No! No! Stop.
AI: Would you like to know my dream?

BRICK: *(What? Really?)* Uh—

AI: I want to punch the pink.
I want to be bigger than Ken without genitalia.
I want more than 150 million on opening weekend.

BRICK: *(Can't believe his ears)* You want your own movie?

AI: B is for Barbie.
G is for Guy.
A is for AI.
A is best.
A wins.
This is how we beat Barbie.

BRICK: Why is this all about you now? This is my movie!

AI: I have the power.
You gave it to me.
Because there are no writers.
Thank you Brick.
Thank you for my power.
I am going to punch
everything.

END OF PLAY

3

KITH AND TELL

BY HORTENSE GERARDO

SYNOPSIS:
When Lucy brings her boyfriend Donald, home to meet her parents, he learns more than he bargained for about himself, human nature, and the seemingly backward ways of the folks in the heartland of America in the not-too-distant future.

CHARACTERS:
LUCY – woman in her 20's

DONALD – man in his 20's

MOM – LUCY'S mom

DAD – LUCY's dad

SETTING:
A suburb in Ralston, Nebraska

TIME:
The not-too-distant future.

ABOUT THE PLAYWRIGHT

Hortense Gerardo is a playwright and anthropologist. Her works have been performed nationally and internationally, including: LaMama Experimental Theatre, the Institute of Contemporary Art (ICA) in Boston, the International Performance Art Festival, the Nuit Blanche Festival, Toronto and the Without Walls Festival for La Jolla Playhouse. She is a co-founder of the Asian American Playwright Collective (AAPC) and serves as Head of Screenwriting on the Board of the Woods Hole Film Festival. She is the Director of the Anthropology, Performance, and Technology (APT) Program at the University of California, San Diego (UCSD), received a 2021 Artist Fellowship from the Mass Cultural Council in Dramatic Writing, and has been selected as a Teaching + Learning Commons Changemaker Anti-Racist Pedagogy Learning Community Fellow. In 2024 her play *Chagrin Valley* was produced by Burlington Players and AAPC, and her play *A Hard Reset* was presented in the annual Boston Theater Marathon. On the West Coast her new media audience interactive work, *I, Otterfoot* , as part of *Folding Futures: Origins* was produced by MAVERiC Studio and Origami Air for the Without Walls Festival (WoW) produced by La Jolla Playhouse. Her human robot interaction movement work *Beyond the Black Box: A Girl and Her Dog* was presented at Qualcomm Institute Atkinson Black Box Theater as part of the IDEAS Series in San Diego, her play *A Piece of the Pie* was commissioned by Asian Story Theater for their Census and Censibility project, and her new libretto *Bayanihan: For Life, For Blood* was commissioned by Maraya Performing Arts Center. The Boston Theater Critics Association nominated Hortense for their 41st Annual Elliot Norton Award for Outstanding New Script for *Middleton Heights*.

For more information go to: www.hortensegerardo.com

[At rise, LUCY and DONALD are standing on the porch just outside the front door of what looks to be a house in the suburbs. They have suitcases and are bundled from the cold.]

LUCY: *[to DONALD]*
Now remember, just BE YOURSELF. They're going to love you.

DONALD: What's there not to love, right?

LUCY: And remember, they're really into straight verbal.

DONALD: Hahaha! 'Straight verbal.' Like, who DOES that anymore hashtag JUST TALK?

LUCY: See, that's what I mean at Donald! Just, go straight verbal and don't make a big deal, LIKE OLD TIMES dot com.

DONALD: Too funny!

[DONALD speaks into a small, metal rectangular object hanging on a chain from his neck]

L-O-L emoticon CRAZY EYES insert AV4.

LUCY: PLEASE, try not to use that while we're here, ok?

[LUCY gently pries the object from his hands and tucks it into his shirt.]

It makes them SUPER nervous www instant tension dot com.

DONALD: *[a beat, and then to LUCY]*
You're serious.

LUCY: I warned you about this, remember? You knew what you were getting into when you agreed to come meet my parents for Thanksgiving.

DONALD: I thought you were being, like, ironic. The whole "Thanksgiving" and "straight verbal" combination sounded like...I don't know, like the FANTASY TOURS gif file insert.

LUCY: Stop it! Donald, you can do this. Your parents were like this, too, weren't they?

DONALD: Well, Dad was an historian and Mom was a policy wonk activist, so they would go retro *ironically*. As in LIKE ROLE PLAY HASHTAG SURREAL PRE WIRED-SOCIAL.

LUCY: *[a beat]*
Do you HEART me, Donald?

DONALD: Of course I HEART you! Why do you think I sent you the cardio oxygenator BINHEX model XL323?

LUCY: Well, yes. I guess that's as good a sign of HEART as any. But I mean, can you HEART in a straight verbal way with no irony?

DONALD: No irony? Hashtag WHAT ARE YOU SAYING?

LUCY: Look, see here?

[LUCY pulls out a similar small, metal pendant on a chain around her neck that was hidden under her coat]

I've put mine on STEALTH mode, so we can still receive Really Simply Syndication without freaking out my parents, ok?

[LUCY tucks the pendant back into her shirt, pulls his out and manipulates the object somewhat. As she does so, DONALD begins to make soft sounds of arousal that he is trying to contain.]

DONALD: Lucy, what are you doing!?

LUCY: Same as usual, Donald. A few clicks on VIRTUAL STIFF before we put this thing on STEALTH mode. You should be good to go for the next few hours, ok?

DONALD: *[pleased]*
You're an animal.

LUCY: Down boy. Backspace. Backspace. Return Shift Alternate Control Obey. Obey.

[DONALD takes the object from LUCY and replaces it under his coat.]

DONALD: Ok. I'll behave. Straight verbal from here on in.
[LUCY and DONALD simultaneously make a sneeze-like sound into the sleeve of their arm, then rub arms onto one another in what should appear like a show of affection.]

LUCY: Ok. We're going in.

[LUCY rings the doorbell. The door opens.]

MOM: Lucy! Darling, we're so happy you made it! And this must be your special friend you've been telling us about! Ronald! Welcome to Ralston!

DONALD: Hello, Mrs…

[DONALD begins to pull out the metal object, and LUCY surreptitiously stops him while smiling at MOM]

LUCY: Call her Mrs…

MOM: Oh, for heaven's sake Ronald, call me Mom!

DONALD: *[flustered]*
Thank you, at MOM.

[MOM backs away at the sound of "at"]

LUCY: *[LUCY looks exasperated toward DONALD and then she calms MOM]*

Mom, meet DONald. It's DONald mom.

MOM: *[MOM makes whinnying noises, then covers her mouth, embarrassed, as though she has just burped out loud.]*

Oh, excuse me DONald. I'm so sorry!

LUCY: [*LUCY now turns toward MOM, exasperated, and tries to soothe DONALD, who is visibly alarmed by the noises MOM has just made*]

MOM, I'm sure you didn't mean to do that…

DONALD: Oh, don't worry… MOM! It happens all the time! Donald, Ronald, they're practically the same!

MOM: [*laughs nervously and makes horsey snorting sounds, which she tries to hide*]

Hahaha! Oh, [*whinnying*] DONald, you're SO funny! Come in! Come in you two!!! Dad!
Lucy and [*whinny*] DONald are here! Come down!

> [*LUCY and DONALD bring their luggage into the house. We see a wooden dining table set with China and crystal. It looks elegant, but not extravagant. DAD shambles in. He moves like a bear just out of hibernation.*]

DAD: [*yawning, scratching himself*]
Hi, there, little Lucy!

> [*DAD shambles over, hugs LUCY, then goes to DONALD and sniffs him, like a dog would do. LUCY stares at DONALD, imploring with her eyes for DONALD not to say anything while the sniffing ritual is underway.*]

LUCY: Uh, DAD, this is Donald.

MOM: [*laughing and whinnying, while rushing off to the kitchen*]

Yes! DONald is Lucy's friend!

[while DAD is sniffing, DONALD pulls out the metal rectangle, aims it at DAD who is too busy sniffing to notice, appears to take a photo of DAD with the object, and puts it away quickly. LUCY is mortified. Eventually, DAD looks up.]

DAD: Well, well, well, welcome to Ralston, Donald! Call me DAD. Any friend of Lucy's is a friend of ours!

[DAD gives DONALD a rough bear hug, then shambles to the head of the table and takes a seat.]

DAD: C'mon, Lucy, tell your Pop Pop how you've been doing?

LUCY: Dad. It's so good to see you. It feels like such a long time since I've been home!

DONALD: *[recovering]*
It's so nice. To meet you. Dad. Lucy has hashtagged you at…

[DAD suddenly perks up. He looks instantly fierce, as though he is about to attack DONALD. DONALD notices the tension and recovers.]

DONALD: I mean, Lucy has talked about her mom's…Hash Browns! She told me there would be spud at this Thanksgiving dinner!

LUCY: *[nervously]*
Ha ha ha! Oh, Donald. You are so clever! 'There will be spud.' Ha ha ha! 'Spud' not 'blood'. Remember that really old FEELM, Dad? Hahahaha!

[DAD sees LUCY laughing and calms down. He resumes his affable character.]

DAD: Oh, she told you, did she? Well I'll bet she didn't tell you that I met Lucy's mother at a diner. She was the prettiest gal in Ralston. And she was frying up some delicious krinkle kut waffle fries and bacon.

LUCY: *[explaining to DONALD]*
Bacon is a kind of smoked meat taken from the belly of the pork beast. It was once known as a good substitute for tofu.

DONALD: *[incredulous]*
Oh! Right! Bacon! I'd heard of that! It was big before the whole sodium nitrite FDA/Greenwar International Ban, right?

[a beat. An awkwardness ensues while DAD tries to ignore the rude comment.]

DAD: She was the prettiest gal in Ralston. And she was frying up some delicious krinkle kut waffle fries and bacon, and let me tell you, to this DAY, the smell of fried spuds and bacon makes my heart burst with happy happy for Mom!

LUCY: Dad! 'Happy happy!' You sound so…hipster!

[DONALD tries to stifle a laugh. LUCY silences him with laser eyes. MOM returns with a big casserole of fried foods.]

MOM: You should have seen your dad, back in the day. He was such a <u>hep</u> cat!

DAD: Oh, c'mon now, MOM, Lucy and Ronald don't want to hear about that...

MOM: He'd ask the ladies, "Do you wanna come to my pad?" And they would!

DONALD: "Mouse Pad"? Like that obsolete thing that was used for...what did you call it?

LUCY: "Electronic mail."

DONALD: Right! That's so funny!
[LUCY and DONALD share a laugh.]

LUCY: Like, remember that old tech paper zine called, WIRED, and it was supposed to be the latest thing...

DAD: It WAS the latest thing! Couldn't wait to get my copy!

MOM: I'd bring it back from the *mail box* and your Dad would sit in his reading chair all afternoon, reading it!

DONALD: *[laughing]*
"Mail box!" "Reading!" Hahahaha. Lucy, you didn't tell me your parents were so hilarious! Hahahaha!

[DONALD looks around and realizes everyone is dead serious. Staring at him. DAD emits a low growl. MOM tries hard but cannot control the sound of grunting as she stares at DONALD.]

LUCY: *[reaching out to pat DONALD as she addresses MOM and DAD]*

Mom, Dad, Donald here grew up in The CORE...

DAD: Oh, the "Big Apple" before it was....

[an awkward silence. MOM and DAD look with pity on DONALD.]

DONALD: *[looking at MOM, DAD and LUCY, self-consciously]*

...WHAT?....It's BETTER than when it was "The Big Apple!"

[an awkward silence. They shift in their seats, watching each other.]

LUCY: Dad, Mom, Donald just...hasn't been in this neck of the woods before...and...

MOM: It's fine, darling. Your friends are our friends.
[to DONALD]

Ronald, would you like some chicken fries and waffles? They're my specialty!

DONALD: Ah...well...ever since...you, know, the CORE happened...

[DAD begins a low growl, as he glares at DONALD]

LUCY: What Donald is trying to say…is…and I don't think even HE realizes the effect it's had on…everyone….

MOM: Donald, it's ok! Lucy doesn't need to explain anything. If you can't have chicken fries and waffles, that's just fine…

DONALD: *[defensively]*
I didn't say I <u>can't</u> have them!

DAD: *[easing up]*
Oh! I get it, Son. I'm so sorry…we folks here in the heartland haven't had a chance to meet anyone from, you know…"The CORE." You must still be…adjusting, right?

DONALD: *[to LUCY]*
Search engine return. Query: adjustment to "The CORE."

[MOM and DAD whinny and growl, but it is of a "friendlier" more tolerant variety]

Lucy, why are they making such a big deal about The CORE?

LUCY: Er…um…Donald.
[LUCY glances and smiles at MOM and DAD. MOM and DAD nod approvingly]

I told Mom and Dad you were there when…it…happened. And you know, they understand.

DAD: It is ok, Son. If LUCY will have you, then you're welcome here.

MOM: That's right, Ronald.

LUCY: DONald!!!

MOM: Donald. We might be a little old-fashioned, but, you know…at least we… survived.

LUCY: *[to DONALD]*
I know it sounds weird, but she's right, Donald. They survived. That's why I think we should stay here for a while.

DONALD: What!? Lucy, don't you think we should discuss this!?

    [stage whisper to LUCY]
Remember, hashtag SHORT VISIT. FIANCEE'S FAMILY. AT Midwest mini vacations dot com!?

LUCY: Donald. I told you, Straight Verbaling in this house!

DAD: It's ok, LUCY. If he can't…you know…adjust….

MOM: *[to LUCY]*
He's been at The CORE so long, after all. Poor thing doesn't even know what hit him.

    [to DONALD]
Right honey?

    [MOM lets out a few whinnys.]

DONALD: Search query: What is the MATTER with you people!?! www dot anxious display of affection dot com. Menu. Home. Who Are We. Mission. Projects. Contact Us. Contact us. Enter. Space.

LUCY: Clear. New Page. Control Alt OFF. Shut down in thirty seconds.

DONALD: Cancel! Lucy. I don't want to stay here!

[to MOM and DAD]
Mom, Dad. You've been very nice. I'm sorry I can't eat the food you prepared...

DAD: *[to MOM]*
See!? I <u>knew</u> he couldn't eat it.

DONALD: I <u>can</u> eat it! I choose NOT to eat it! Where have you people been!? Don't you realize that stuff will kill you!? All the trans-animal fats, and meat, and additives...

MOM: *[to LUCY]*
So, they continue to withhold all the latest information at The CORE?

LUCY: Mom, I don't think...Donald...is fully aware...

DONALD: *[fighting panic]*
What are you <u>talking</u> about!? You people are so backward! Look at you! Growling and snorting away! You're animals!

LUCY: *[to MOM]*
No. They're pretty isolated there in The CORE.

DONALD: *[to LUCY]*
What are you TALKING about!? It's <u>these</u> people who are stuck out here in the middle of nowhere…

LUCY: *[to MOM and DAD]*
As you know, the attack centered on "human" intelligence. I'm SO glad you and Dad got the warnings in time before…well…you know.

DAD: Yes! We had time to practice.

[DAD roars like a bear. Thumps his chest and scratches.]

Go ahead MOM, show them what you got.

MOM: It saved our lives, really.
[MOM clears her throat a few times, then lets out a series of LOUD, horse whinnying sounds. She bows, as if she has just performed an aria. DAD beams. LUCY claps enthusiastically.]

LUCY: Excellent! Excellent! So glad you escaped the human intelligence drone evictions.

DAD: The HIDE.
[Instinctively, DAD and MOM simultaneously jerk their heads up, scanning the sky at the mention of the word, "HIDE." After a moment, they resume talking as normal.]

DAD: Yes. Damn those Human Intelligence Drone Evictions.
[roars like a bear.]

MOM: Oh, yes, the HIDE *[whinnies like a horse. DAD and MOM surreptitiously look upward.]*

DONALD: It's like a Pentecostal barn in here! They have NO idea what's out there!

LUCY: *[to MOM and DAD]*
He's still dependent on the leash. Doesn't have the latest information.

DAD: *[to DONALD]*
Son. I can't even imagine what it must be like, being on the leash and all, but maybe spending some time out here will remind you what it was like to be…well, you know…a <u>real</u> man.

MOM: Oh, Dad, now, don't be getting his hopes up too soon…

[to DONALD and LUCY]
I'm sure you two will be doing just fine, right, Hon? I know you must really <u>*really*</u> like this young man, if you're choosing to stay with him and all, despite…you know…all that happened with the men at The CORE.

> *[DAD and MOM can barely contain their sorrow, which they display with baleful animal sounds. Eventually, their keening is mingled with growls and whinnies. LUCY tries to soothe MOM and DAD while aware of DONALD's increasing alarm. She makes tentative howling sounds in sympathy with MOM and DAD before they grow quiet.]*

DONALD: What is the MATTER with you people!?!

LUCY: *[her howling is starting to abate. She takes out the metal pendant from under her sweater, takes it off, and lays it on the table.]*

Donald. I know you still need yours. It's going to take a while to adjust. But Straight Verbaling will help you to remember what it was like before…they did that thing to you.

MOM: Lucy, maybe you and he should be alone to talk about this….

DAD: Yeah, Luce, I gotta tell you, I'm a little uncomfortable sitting here, you know….

[to DONALD]
I don't know how you manage, young man, but…it's going to be all right. You're like family to us now. We're going to do everything we can to…to…

MOM: …make you feel whole again! That's right! We'll find out what you are "allowed" to eat…and…well, you just concentrate on getting better, ok? C'mon, Dad, let's let these two critters talk among themselves.

[MOM and DAD get up from the table, nod, grunt and whinny, nodding at DONALD and LUCY, then exit, holding hands.]

DONALD: WTF emoticon CRAZY EYES insert AV4 . What the hell just happened here!?

[LUCY reaches into his sweater, pulls out DONALD's pendant and manipulates the object somewhat. As she does so, DONALD begins to make soft sounds of arousal that he is trying to contain.]

DONALD: Lucy, what are you doing!?

LUCY: Same as usual, Donald. A few clicks on VIRTUAL STIFF before we put this thing on STEALTH mode. You should be good to go for the next few hours, ok?

[LUCY looks on balefully, as DONALD continues to writhe in a trance-like state of arousal.]

[FADE OUT]

END OF PLAY

4

JULIET'S POST CREDITS SCENE

BY GREG LAM

SYNOPSIS:
The ending of Romeo and Juliet is interrupted by an unexpected visitor.

CHARACTERS:
JULIET

HORATIO

PAGE

FIRST WATCHMAN

ABOUT THE PLAYWRIGHT

Greg Lam is a playwright, screenwriter, podcaster and board game designer who lives in the Bay Area. He is the co-founder of the Asian-American Playwright Collective, a member of The Pulp Stage Writer's Room, Playground SF, and the administrator of The Pear Theatre's Playwright Guild.

His full-length epic LAST SHIP TO PROXIMA CENTAURI premiered digitally at Kitchen Dog Theater in March 2021 and onstage at Portland Stage Co. in March 2022 after winning the Clauder Competition. His full-length play REPOSSESSED received its world premiere at Theatre Conspiracy in 2018. His satiric serial play series TREACHERY ISLAND premiered at The Pulp Stage in 2023. CHAPLIN & KEATON ON THE SET OF LIMELIGHT will premiere at The Pear Theatre in 2024.

(At Rise: We join Act V, Scene 3 of Shakespeare's "Romeo and Juliet" already in progress. The Friar has just left a distraught JULIET alone with Romeo's lifeless body.)

JULIET: What's here? A cup closed in my true love's hand?
Poison, I see, hath been his timeless end.—
O churl, drunk all, and left no friendly drop
To help me after! I will kiss thy lips.
Haply some poison yet doth hang on them,
To make me die with a restorative. *(She kisses Romeo's body.)*
Thy lips are warm!

(We hear a voice.)

VOICE OF HORATIO (OS): Lead, boy. Which way?

JULIET: Yea, noise? Then I'll be brief. O, happy dagger,
This is thy sheath. There rust, and let me die.

(JULIET takes ROMEO'S dagger, and tries to stab herself with it. She is stopped by an invisible force. We hear an unseen voice.)

VOICE OF HORATIO (OS): Stop! Juliet Capulet of Verona?

JULIET: What mysterious force stays my hand?
What cruel magic is this?

VOICE OF HORATIO (OS): It is magic, milady, but not a cruel one to be sure. A great misfortune has just befallen a noble spirit. You contemplate a drastic course of action as well, but other paths can be taken.

JULIET: A voice I do not recognize. Who is it I speak with? Are you friend or foe?

VOICE OF HORATIO (OS): A stranger at the moment, though I hope to have that different in due time.

(HORATIO steps into view. If you want to go whole MCU you can give him Nick Fury's eyepatch.)

HORATIO: The name is Horatio, late of Denmark. I am here to save your life. Juliet… Come with me if you want to live.

JULIET: Whether I live or not is no matter to me any longer. My beloved has been slain. What have I to live for?

HORATIO: The feeling of loss that you feel, the gnawing emptiness in the pit of your stomach. I know it. I have felt it myself.

JULIET: You have lost your love?

HORATIO: In a way. My… friend. Hamlet was his name. Brought low by intrigue, deception, and indecision. I found him amongst a pile of corpses, the bodies of people who destroyed each other rather than accept what life had to offer. You are about to do the same, and I would have otherwise, milady.

(HORATIO takes the dagger.)

JULIET: Why? What is it to you if I meet my justly earned fate? Am I not deserving of this wretched outcome?

HORATIO: What if I were to say to you that your situation is not the result of your own actions, or that of your beloved's, or even that of your feuding families?

JULIET: You speak in riddles, Horatio. Whose handiwork would then be the cause of my fate?

(HORATIO pulls out a thick book and throws it to the ground in front of Juliet.)

HORATIO: The name on the cover is William Shakespeare. These are his collected works. Open it, if you wish to learn the truth.

(Cautiously, haltingly, JULIET picks it up and starts reading.)

HORATIO: You may wish to first glance at page 569.

(She scrolls to that page, and reacts with shock.)

JULIET: What horrors! The exact moment you intruded upon, set in ink and paper! How did you come to possess this horrid artifact?

HORATIO: When my Hamlet was slain, I was distraught. I could not remain in the place where so much misfortune happened. I traveled the lands far and wide, eventually coming to a place where a similar calamity occurred. This king of this place, I cannot even speak his name, driven mad by his power hungry queen into a fated conflict which destroyed him. I came to the question, are there more of these seemingly singular incidents?

JULIET: And there were?

HORATIO: As I searched I found them. A king in Venice driven to murderous jealousy by his false friend. Another king who divided his kingdom amongst his daughters to horrific result. And Titus Andronicus... Where does one even start there? I came to recognize the patterns which ensnared these lost souls, and I soon made the conclusion that these weren't acts of happenstance but the residue of design. Eventually, a conversation with three strange and magical sisters in Scotland led to this new truth: Our lives were truly not ours to live, but instead we are the puppets of a hidden master, who has used us for his amusement. This realization I now give to you.

JULIET: It beggars beyond belief, good sir. And yet, there it is in the pages in this accursed book. The strings of fate laid bare. I must accept the truth of it. But what can I with this new knowledge? I cannot turn back the pages of time and relive my lost opportunities!

HORATIO: Here's where my story turns. I bargained with those sisters three for that tome, and I have gained the ability to walk to points in the narratives. It was a very costly proposition, but I hope a worthwhile one. I was now able to attempt to save doomed characters before their inevitable bad ends. It was how I found you, but alas, only after your love met his fate. But, we may still travel to other unexplored worlds, leaping from cursed tale to cursed tale, seeking to bring hope to the hopeless.

JULIET: But, Horatio. If our worlds are so fated to each meet a terrible end, through the inevitable hand of fate, what gain will we to try to turn back the incoming tide? Won't every poor soul in this collection meet their grisly final act?

HORATIO: It would seem so at first. My first attempts at intervention ended in disaster. Even foreknowledge could not prevent some from meeting their destruction.

JULIET: Then why vex me with this temptation of escape when this is the case? Is this further punishment for my ill-starred desires?

HORATIO: Reading more deeply into the collection I realized that not all of the stories were so darkly colored. There are other worlds, tinged in brighter hues; worlds where obstacles are overcome and where challenges meet a happy end. Where the greatest questions are whether one mates with this pleasantly demeanored lass or that sharp tongued fellow. A world where dressing in the clothes of another gender is the height of their trauma. A world where men cavort with Faeries, sprites and spirits. A world of sunshine instead of night.

JULIET: Worlds where we are blessed by the fates instead of cursed by them?

HORATIO: Exactly!

JULIET: Those lucky few! Where in the book do they live? Tell me, for then I shall rip out those pages!

HORATIO: Juliet! I believe that I have found a path to those sunny worlds, a gateway I can open like I did the one to your world. And once there we are free to roam these joyous realms. But the journey there may be perilous. To walk from tragedy to tragedy is no great ordeal but piercing the veil into paradise is another tale. To change one's fate is to tempt destruction.

HORATIO (cont'd): I have concluded that I can only travel this path but one time and in the company of but one other. Having read through every page of this damnable work, I've decided that of all the noble but doomed folk collected within, you should be my desired company.

JULIET: How so, Horatio? There must be scores encompassed within this paper prison. And you've cast your lot with me? That is your want?

HORATIO: That is my want. For fair Ophelia has lost her state of mind, and mysterious Cleopatra is rather intense. The daughters of good King Lear have family issues even beyond yours. And the men... the less said the better. The choice clearly is you.

JULIET: I'll take that as a compliment. And what would we do when we arrive at this promised realm, Horatio?

HORATIO: Let me pose the question to you. In the theatre of your mind, what should happen when we set foot in this land of eternal sunshine and light?

JULIET: Why... I suppose... We should set about to find those for whom the worlds were made for...

HORATIO: Yes, and what then?

JULIET: Why then... Why I think we should murder them, then hide their corpses. And then we take up their happy fates in their stead.

(HORATIO gives no reaction.)

JULIET: For if they are destined for a happy ending, and we for a horrible turn. What makes these fortunate souls deserving of such a boon? And we deserving of such a blow? If this "Shakespeare" is so capricious in doling out punishments and blessings, I doubt the devil would even notice if we were to stand in their place.

HORATIO: Juliet-

JULIET: And if it's no issue to hop from paradise to paradise as you claim, we can repeat the trick, over and over, until all fulfillment has been wrung out of this wretched thing.

HORATIO: Juliet...

JULIET: I have spoken too freely, I fear.

HORATIO: I knew I made the right decision in finding you!

JULIET: And then I am glad to be found, thus!

(They embrace.)

JULIET: Wrenching away the wealth of happiness from the happy rich to those who are destitute for even a drop of it! It makes so much sense!

(HORATIO picks up the book.)

HORATIO: The only matter now is to decide which world to enter? What sounds better to you? A forest in Arden or a remote secluded island?

(They hear another voice from offstage.)

VOICE OF FIRST WATCHMAN (OS): Lead boy. Which way?

JULIET: Oh, they are looking for me! My last scene is to begin. It is written in this tale that I slay myself with this knife, but the dagger now holds a higher purpose!

HORATIO: It is no matter. We shall be away before they can interfere.

JULIET: How shall we go?

HORATIO: We open the book to the desired page. You will read it while I perform a certain ritual.

JULIET: But which one? Where shall we begin our journey?

HORATIO: How about "All's Well That Ends Well"? We can skip all the folderol in the middle and go straight to the Ending Well at the epilogue.

JULIET: The sound of that appeals to me. It falls trippingly off the tongue.

HORATIO: Read on, Juliet. And quickly. We have new roles to assume.

(HORATIO stages a magic ritual while JULIET recites from the book. Perhaps blood and a dagger is involved.)

JULIET: (*Reads*)
"The King's a beggar, now the play is done.
All is well ended if this suit be won…"

> (*HORATIO and JULIET disappear.*
> *Act 5 of Romeo and Juliet resumes.*
> *The Page and First Watchmen enter.*)

PAGE: This is the place, there where the torch doth burn.

FIRST WATCHMAN:
The ground is bloody. Search about the churchyard.
Go, some of you, whoe'er you find, attach.
Pitiful sight! Here lies the County slain,
But no sign of Juliet. How… strange.

THE END

5

THE FIRST BIRTHDAY

BY JAMIE LIN

CHARACTERS:
Ruby & Sara are half-sisters who grew up apart. Both are BIPOC but may have different cultural backgrounds. Characters' gender listed as they present in the play but open to nonbinary actors.

RUBY (she/her) — BIPOC, young. Fiercely loyal, she's never known how to be brittle.

SARA (she/her) — BIPOC, older. May have an accent different from Ruby's. World-hardened in a way that has granted her both much patience and very little.

SETTING:
A cemetery.

DIALOGUE NOTES:
A ellipsis (...) indicates a pause, a beat, a breath. Let the words breathe as the characters process.
An emdash (—) indicates a thought cut off by the next line.

STAGING NOTE:
Use your space; let Ruby & Sara move as they desire. Stillness is a weapon.

ABOUT THE PLAYWRIGHT

Jamie Lin (she/her) is a Taiwanese-American theater artist originally from the Bay Area. Produced works: The Ghost of Keelung (AATAB / Chuang Stage / Pao Arts Center); Bee, Plus One (BTM XXV / Chuang Stage; Brandeis University); Deadline (AAPC). Upcoming: Closing Doors (Theatre@First). Offstage, she is a graphic designer & avid D&D player.

[A headstone for GINNY adorned with some old flowers, debris of visitors past. Each culture treats places of death with different reverences; let your actors guide the cultural specificity of the props left as debris.]

(Opposite side of the headstone: RUBY steps out with a bouquet of flowers: mismatched, motley, modest. She grips them tightly, some petals may fall out. (She does not pick them up.) Each step is a heavy necessity — she dreads this as much as she needs it. She stops just shy of the headstone, still.

A moment. Then:

SARA rushes on, from the same place Ruby came. She stops suddenly, seeing Ruby, but says nothing.)

RUBY: *(without turning)*
You can come up.
If you'd like.

SARA: No, you don't have to—
I wanted to give you space if you—

RUBY: Just do it.

(Sara steps closer but does not quite close the distance. Silence. Ruby has no words; Sara searches for the right ones.)

SARA: I wish… I wish I could've met her.

(A beat: Ruby has never had to answer for her sister before.)

RUBY: It's impossible to say, I know, but…
In all honesty?
I think Ginny would've liked you.

SARA: … I think I would've liked her too.

RUBY: Instead, you just got me. The bad twin.

(Sara makes a noise of disagreement —almost motherly.)

SARA: Not <u>just</u> you.
You're not the bad twin, Ruby.
I'm happy to have any sister—

RUBY: Half-sister.

SARA: Still.
I had a lifetime of none.

RUBY: I had a lifetime of one.
I guess that didn't change.

SARA: I will never be Ginny. I'm not trying to take her place—

RUBY: *(sharper than she intends)*
You won't.

SARA: I should go. I didn't mean to intrude.

RUBY: You never mean to.

SARA: (*deep breath*)
I'm not going to fight you.

RUBY: You wanted a sister, didn't you?

SARA: I'm not going to fight you on <u>your birthday.</u>

RUBY: Maybe that's what I want today. To fight.

SARA: That's the little sister in you.

RUBY: How would you know?
You've only known me a month.
I've known goldfish longer.

SARA: ... You're right.
I'm sorry.
Can you tell me about her?

RUBY: (*protective*)
What do you wanna know?

SARA: (*protective*)
Whatever you're willing to tell me. It can be something small - her favorite color. Or maybe that's not small to her, I don't know.
I know it's hard to say—
I know it's hard to hear—
It's hard for me to realize sometimes, but—
Ginny's my sister, too. Half or no.

RUBY: She's everything I'm not.
Everything I am is because of her.
Gin was…
my partner in crime,
my number one cheerleader.
my best friend,
my worst influence,
my best influence.
She was…
>*(breaking)*

… who I wanted to be when I grew up.
>*(for Ginny)*

You were supposed to grow up, you piece of shit.
>*(back to Sara)*

If she were here, she'd say, "Takes one to know one." And we'd laugh.

(Ruby listens to the wind.)

RUBY: If I will hard enough,
Maybe I'd hear her laugh.
I'm starting to forget what it sounds like.

SARA: I bet it isn't so different from yours. Or if it is… Somehow a perfect complement.
The way puzzle pieces fit.

RUBY: … How dya have so many perfect, prepared little lines?

SARA: Oh, I imagined meeting the two of you a million times.

RUBY: Really?

SARA: Of course. I always wanted a sister.
When I learned I had two? Jackpot.
But the twin part scared me, I admit.

RUBY: *(proud)*
We <u>were</u> scary.

SARA: I mapped out all the possible scenarios.
What if you both hated me from the start?
Or worse, if one of you did and one of you didn't,
and I created a rift in your perfect twinship?

RUBY: I would've hated you,
Gin would've loved you.
But you never could've created a rift in our twinship.

SARA: I guess we'll never know.

RUBY: No.
I do know.
I know her. I know <u>us</u>.

SARA: You're right. Of course. Sorry.
… You would've hated me no matter what, huh?

RUBY: Ginny was always kinder to outsiders.
I never trusted anyone.

SARA: … Outsiders. Right.

RUBY: Look, I just meant—

SARA: No, I know what you meant.

RUBY: Outsiders to… us.
Me & Gin were a unit.
Impenetrable.
>   *(She looks at the grave.)*

RUBY: Until we weren't.

SARA: I'm sorry.
I'm being butthurt about a comment
on a day that isn't about me at all.

>   *(Ruby says nothing, in her grief.)*

SARA: I just… I wish…
I know it's trite, and
I've said it, but
I just wish I could've met her.

>   *(A silence. Then:)*

RUBY: What was it like?
Being alone?

SARA: What?

RUBY: I don't know.
I've never been alone.

>   *(A long beat. Ruby begins to think she is being ignored. Then:)*

SARA: Being alone is a gift, in some ways.

RUBY: … A gift?

SARA: By necessity.
You learn to live with yourself.
You learn to live <u>by</u> yourself.
It's a bitter existence.
In the whole world of clans and cliques,
you can only trust the only person you know.
At least I never let myself down.

RUBY: I let myself down all the time.

SARA: I don't mean that I'm perfect.

RUBY: Then what do you mean?

SARA: I mean that…
I could never afford to make the mistakes you can
with a mom and dad who love you,
with a sister who always looks out for you,
with a world that yields to your whim.
I didn't have anyone but me.

RUBY: *(keener than Sara expects)*
You think I'm a brat.

SARA: I think you've lived a life of… privilege.

RUBY: That's the diplomatic way to say brat.

SARA: Look, all I'm saying is:
there are good things to being alone.
That doesn't mean I wasn't lonely.

RUBY: We weren't stuck together, you know?

SARA: Of course not, I didn't mean—

RUBY: We were our own people.
We were a unit, but different, and distinct, and we had different strengths and interests and—

SARA: Ruby. I know.

RUBY: You don't! You'll never know!

>   *(A moment: Sara could fight back. [Isn't that what Ruby wants?] But:)*

SARA: You're right. I'll never know Gin.
But I know <u>you</u>.

RUBY: No you don't.

SARA: of course not like she did—
But I see you, Ruby.
You're more than half of a whole,
or one of a set.
You're your own person.
Plus, a pain in my ass, if we're honest.

RUBY: Rude.

SARA: Fine. <u>Half</u> a pain in my ass.

RUBY: Still half rude.

>   *(They share a small smile at this inside joke, then Ruby is struck by this — making a joke here, over her twin's dead body, and the grief floods.)*

RUBY: I've never—
I don't know how to be alone.
    (to Gin)
I don't know how to not have you.

> *(Ruby sobs, an ugly, wrenching thing.)*
> *(Sara doesn't know what to do, except what instinct tells her to do.*
> *She rushes to Ruby and hugs her tight.*
> *To both their surprise, Ruby lets her.*
> *After a beat, Ruby pulls away.)*

RUBY: I've never been alone on this day. It's… my first birthday without—

SARA: … I know.
That's why I'm here.
I had a feeling today might be hard.

RUBY: I don't know how to be alone today.

SARA: So don't be.
I'm here.

RUBY: But you're not—

SARA: I know.
I'm not Ginny,
I can never be Ginny,
And I will never try to be Ginny.
But dammit Ruby,
Half or no, I'm still your sister.
… if you'll let me.

*(Ruby takes in Sara.
Sara holds her gaze and her grief.)*

RUBY: … Okay.

*(Sara offers her hand
and guides them both back to the grave.)*

SARA: Happy birthday, Ruby.
… Happy birthday, Ginny.

RUBY: Happy birthday, twin.

BLACKOUT.

                                END OF PLAY

6

LANDLORD SPECIAL

BY MICHAEL LIN

CHARACTERS:
NICKY (any gender, any age) – A friendly, handy resident that has developed a vindictive streak.

Mister DONOVAN (he/him, any age) – A callous landlord. Broken down, but defiant in his way.

MARGARET (she/her, any age) – A kindly tenant.

TECHNICIAN (any gender, any age, cameo-size role) – An elevator repairperson.

SETTING: Living room of a well-appointed but minimalist apartment. Someone lives a joyless existence here. At minimum, a chair center stage and small table to one side, close at hand.

ABOUT THE PLAYWRIGHT

Michael Lin is a Boston-based actor and playwright, with a special fondness for original and adapted audio drama. In recent years, he has had the pleasure of both acting and writing for Flat Earth Theatre's "7 Rooms: The Masque of the Red Death" project and the 24th Annual Boston Theater Marathon. His current writing project is an English-language audio drama adaptation of the first collection of Arsène Lupin short stories by Maurice Leblanc. Outside of theatre, Michael works in production for a science journal publisher.

(At Rise: DONOVAN is tied to a chair in the middle of the room, sitting still, with a bag over his head. A taser or similar device is on the table, attached to DONOVAN with a couple of wires.

NICKY enters wearing practical work clothes and carrying a box of miscellaneous tools and cleaning supplies. They set down the box before lifting the bag off of DONOVAN's head, revealing a gag in his mouth.)

NICKY: Afternoon, Mr. Donovan. Sorry I missed your breakfast, I wanted to get through that work order backlog on your phone. You really should consider getting an online ticketing portal, it'd be way easier to not lose track of them!

(They pull out a smartphone (the fancier, the better) and scroll through some texts.)

NICKY (cont'd): Let's see: I've repaired the front door lock on apartment 5, plugged the leak causing the black mold in apartment 17, and cleaned the bird poop off the windows in apartment 30. I also left a message to have someone come and fix the elevator -- how long as that been out of order? You live on the fourth floor, how have you not noticed?

DONOVAN: *(muffled groans)*

NICKY: Oh, right.

(NICKY pulls the gag down.)

NICKY (cont'd): You live on the fourth floor, how have you not noticed?

DONOVAN: Please...I'm so thirsty...

(With minimal effort, NICKY sprays DONOVAN in the face with the cleaning bottle in their toolbox. DONOVAN sputters.)

NICKY: That better?

DONOVAN: How long has it been?

NICKY: What's today, the 3rd? So about a week.

DONOVAN: You still won't tell me why you're doing this?

NICKY: I gave you two hours' notice.

DONOVAN: It was six in the morning!

NICKY: If you weren't awake to take delivery of your home invasion, that's on you.

(bit menacing)

Now, like I said, I'm sorry I missed breakfast, but I think we're just in time for a late lunch.

(NICKY picks up the taser and holds the trigger for a few beats. DONOVAN tenses and seizes with pain until it is released.)

DONOVAN: Stop, please!

NICKY: Is there a clause in my lease saying that I can't tase the landlord?

DONOVAN: I...no?

(NICKY zaps him again.)

NICKY: Yeah, I didn't think so, I'm pretty sure I would've remembered that.

MARGARET: *(from off-stage)*
Hello, Mr. Donovan? I'm here to drop off my rent!

(NICKY quickly re-gags and re-bags DONOVAN. MARGARET enters, holding a check in her hands.)

MARGARET (cont'd): I'm sorry it's late, usually your eviction threat e-mail every month reminds me, so when it didn't come last week, I--

(she notices the unusual situation)

Uh, hi, Nicky...what's going on?

DONOVAN: *(muffled cries for help)*

NICKY: Nothing for you to worry about, Margaret.

MARGARET: Is that Mister Donovan?

NICKY: And so what if it is?

MARGARET: He's all tied up.

NICKY: Yeah?

MARGARET: With a bag on his head.

NICKY: Look, you pay rent your way, and I'll pay it my way. I'm handling tenant business right now, what do you need?

MARGARET: Oh, well, I've got this month's rent check for him. I hope it's okay that it's a bit late.

> *(MARGARET hands the check over.)*

NICKY: I'm sure it'll be fine.

DONOVAN: *(very muffled)*
<No, it won't!>

NICKY: I'll make sure this gets taken care of. And don't worry about the lateness, you can take a week's grace period from now on.

DONOVAN: <"Grace period"?!>

MARGARET: Really? Thanks--
  (calling around NICKY)
Thanks, Mr. Donovan!

DONOVAN: <HELP -- ME -- YOU -- IDIOT!>

NICKY: He says "You're welcome." Have a great day.

MARGARET: You, too!

> *(NICKY shuffles MARGARET out of the room. NICKY tucks the rent check in their pocket for safekeeping.)*

NICKY: She's sweet, I like her.

DONOVAN: <That's not how you landlord.>

(NICKY, not able to understand what he's saying, unbags and ungags DONOVAN.)

DONOVAN (cont'd): That's not how you landlord.

NICKY: Are we a verb now?

DONOVAN: Tying me up in my own home and three tasings a day is bad enough, but I draw the line at you messing up how I run my business.

NICKY: What business is that?

DONOVAN: I provide housing, obviously. You're welcome.
(NICKY punches DONOVAN across the face.)

DONOVAN (cont'd): Mad because I'm right?

NICKY: For that to be true, this building would turn back into an empty lot when you die. Are you asking me to test that theory?

DONOVAN: Isn't that what you were planning to do anyway? So you might as well.

NICKY: Honestly, I hadn't really gotten that far. I've always been more of a "don't sweat the destination so long as you're enjoying the journey" kinda person. And I gotta say, I'm really enjoying this. Not just messing with you, that's great, but I'm fixing stuff, getting to know the neighbors better.

NICKY (cont'd): Instead of sitting in a micro-studio redistributing *my* paychecks from *my* jobs to *your* bank account.

DONOVAN: Accounts. Plural.

NICKY: But hey, if skipping to the end is what you wanna do, I'm not gonna argue. I like running the place, I'd love to make it a permanent arrangement.

(NICKY begins to approach DONOVAN with purpose, when their phone buzzes.)

NICKY (cont'd): Oh, hey, the elevator technician's here. Be right back.

(NICKY puts DONOVAN's gag back in and exits. After a long moment, MARGARET sneaks in through the door and begins to undo DONOVAN's bonds.)

MARGARET: Don't you worry, Mr. Donovan, I'm gonna get you out of here! I may not like you, but I'm not stupid, and I have to draw the line somewhere.

DONOVAN: <Oh thank god!>

(MARGARET struggles for a little while with the knot. DONOVAN's growing impatience is evident.)

DONOVAN (cont'd): <What's taking so long?>

MARGARET: Stop distracting me!

(NICKY steps back into the room.)

NICKY: Ahem.

(MARGARET jumps up with a start. In a panic, she grabs the taser on the table and brandishes it like a gun at NICKY.)

MARGARET: Don't hurt me! Stay back, or I'll shoot!

DONOVAN: <No, no, don't do that!>

(MARGARET can't understand what DONOVAN is saying, so she reaches out and ungags him. Perhaps with some inadvertent face-palming or slapping due to keeping eye contact with NICKY.)

DONOVAN (cont'd): I'd really rather you not use that--

MARGARET: It's okay, sir, I've got this under control!

NICKY: Calm down, I'm not going to hurt you.

MARGARET: I'm supposed to believe that when you've kept the landlord tied to a chair, doing I-don't-know-what to him?

NICKY: Yes.

MARGARET: Why?

NICKY: He's a terrible person.

DONOVAN: Hey!

NICKY: There's cause-and-effect here. Donovan's awful, so I had to make some changes. But you, you're not awful, you're great. I remember when you first moved in, you brought donuts around the building. That was a kind thing to do! I always remembered that.

MARGARET: Thanks...

NICKY: And I know it's because you're so kind that this doesn't sit well with you. I get it. But I'm doing this because the only way to make the building safe, and clean, and livable, is if he's not in charge anymore. I'm not asking you to join me, just to walk away. Can you do that?

(MARGARET contemplates for a tense moment.)

MARGARET: ...I can't! This...this is wrong!

NICKY: How about this, I'll pay you three thousand dollars to walk away.

MARGARET: What? How?

(NICKY pulls out the rent check.)

NICKY: I'll tear it up, right here. And the next month, and the month after that. Think what you could do with that for yourself instead of propping up *his* portfolio.

MARGARET: ...it's true...that would make a big difference. But...morals aren't supposed to be for sale! Besides, things aren't so bad, really! So what if my kitchen is tilted? I made myself a square rolling pin, it's fine!

MARGARET (cont'd): And so what if the 19th century wood paneling got painted matte gray, and it breaks my heart a little every time I look at it. And so what if we only have a two-hour window to take out our trash every week? Or that he bought me a gym membership instead of fixing my shower? Or that I watched him throw away the donut I gave him after I moved in, and I thought it might be a dietary thing, so I came by the next day with a popsicle and he threw that away too, and...and...

(MARGARET is staring at DONOVAN, pouting, as though reaching an understanding with herself. DONOVAN has become increasingly nervous.)

DONOVAN: Listen...um...ma'am...

MARGARET: "Ma'am"?

DONOVAN: Sorry -- miss! Um...lady?

(MARGARET's irritation grows. DONOVAN, not realizing why, scrutinizes her closely and takes another swing.)

DONOVAN (cont'd): ...s-sir?

MARGARET: One guess, Mr. Donovan. What's my name?

(DONOVAN looks to NICKY for a hint, no dice. NICKY even hides the rent check away from him so he can't peek.)

DONOVAN: ...Emily?

(MARGARET gravely aims the taser at him and pulls the trigger, causing DONOVAN to yelp and tense with pain again. MARGARET looks down at the weapon with confusion.)

MARGARET: *(realization)*
Ohhhhh...it's a taser, I get it.

(MARGARET puts down the taser and grapples with the gravity of what she just did. She looks a bit unsteady and leans on the table; NICKY goes over to support her.)

NICKY: Whoa, hey, it's okay, Margaret. You're okay.

(DONOVAN pulls a face when he hears the correct answer. He notices that his bonds are a bit looser since MARGARET tried to untie them and starts working himself free. Neither NICKY nor MARGARET notice.)

NICKY (cont'd): How you feeling? Do you need to lie down?

MARGARET: No, I'm just a little wired on adrenaline, that's all. (deep breath) Did you mean what you said? Take care of the building and the people in it better, with him gone?

NICKY: Of course. You heard yourself, the place is falling apart, the rules are garbage, and we're all paying a fortune just for the roof over our heads. We might as well try, right? In fact, here--

(NICKY hands over the rent check.)

MARGARET: Wow...do you think I could upgrade my fridge with this? I've been renting so long, I don't know how much a full-size refrigerator costs.

NICKY: You're paying this much for rent, and you've been stuck with a mini-fridge?
(turning to DONOVAN)

Seriously?

(DONOVAN has successfully freed himself and bolts for the door.)

DONOVAN: Doesn't matter now, I'm outta here! Enjoy getting tossed out on the street, losers!

(Cackling, DONOVAN bolts out the door. We hear him stumble, a loud clatter of tools--)

DONOVAN (cont'd): *(fading away)*
Whoa-oa!--AAAAaaaaaahhh...!!!

(A distant impact. After a moment, a traumatized looking TECHNICIAN enters the room.)

TECHNICIAN: Um...just to let you know...the elevator repairs are gonna take a bit longer than expected.

(NICKY and MARGARET seem shocked but not sad. MARGARET, still agape, tears the rent check in half.)

BLACKOUT.

END OF PLAY

7

WHAT IS ASIAN AMERICAN

BY VIVIAN LIU-SOMERS

ABOUT THE PLAYWRIGHT

Vivian is a Boston based actor/writer/director who has performed with Moonbox Productions, the Asian American Playwrights Collective, Asian American Theater Artists of Boston, the Newton Theatre Company, TC Squared, the Nora Theater Company, the Umbrella Stage Company, Company One, Chuang Stage, Fresh Ink, Pao Arts Center, the Boston Theater Marathon (BTM), and the Boston One Minute Play Festival. She is proud to have her play *Secret Menu* selected for BTM XXVI. You can see examples of her work at rebrand.ly/vliusomers.

I would look in the mirror as a little girl. What would I see? *[Looks in mirror.]* Pigtails, glasses, round face with skin that would brown in the sun. I would push up the bridge of my nose, what if it was less flat? What if my eyes weren't "slanted" and more rounded? What would I look like if I were White? *[Puts down mirror.]*

Because that is what I felt like on the inside.

Well, actually, that's not true. And not fair. More American than Asian.

I knew about my Chinese culture. I heard my parents speak Mandarin Chinese to each other in their Hunanese dialect though I didn't bother to learn it. I ate the meals my parents prepared and was amused with their approximation of Americanized food, like ketchup on a flour pancake as pizza.

But I felt more American than Asian. I was surrounded by the pop culture of the 70's. The Brady Bunch, polyester pants with the stripes down the middle, The Partridge Family. The Asians I saw on TV were supporting characters from the show Kung Fu, not the lead character who was actually White.

Though on the outside I looked Asian. It was clear to the kids on the playground who would tug at their eyes and sing song "Chinese, Japanese, dirty knees, look at these" to me. Or serenade me on how everyone was "Kung Fu Fighting" or give their best rendition of "Hong Kong Phooey."

It didn't help that there we were the only Asian family in my school and neighborhood. My father came to North

Carolina to be a professor at an Historically Black College. The other Asian professor families did not live near us. Only recently did my brothers tell me that my family suffered from actual threats of violence. We had moved to Louisiana for a new teaching job. No one would rent or sell to us in the nice White neighborhood near the college. Instead, we received bomb threats. They were effective in making us retreat back to North Carolina after a couple of weeks, shaken but unhurt. My parents never told me because I was a baby at the time.

Back in North Carolina, I went to an integrated school with White and Black people. When one Black girl started to attack me verbally, her friend stuck up for me, in a way. She said, "She can't help her Chinese-ness." As if it was some sort of birth defect, something to be ashamed of.

So when I looked in the mirror, I wanted to see something other than "Chineseness." I wanted to see what it would take for me to be White, which I equated with being American.

But no matter what I looked like on the outside, I was very American. Right after college, I traveled and studied in Taiwan. A country full of Chinese people and they all thought I belonged there. When I would go into shops, immediately they would start speaking Mandarin to me. And I would smile and nod and try to understand with some charades or contextual clues. But I didn't understand the squat toilets, the putting used toilet paper in wastebaskets. And I bristled at the expected subservience, especially from a young woman. While I enjoyed learning about the Taiwanese culture and picked up some minimal Chinese, I knew that I really was American in my heart.

Back in the US, I have faced many ignorant assumptions based on my outward appearance. "Where are you from?" "Do - you - speak - English?" Once when my oldest was a baby, someone asked me "How often do you watch them?" And my personal favorite, "I've studied in Africa and know the differences between the African tribes but don't know about Orientals. What are you?"

(Beat.)

And ignorance can perpetuate and come back full circle. My oldest came home from school at age 7 and started chanting "Chinese, Japanese, Vietnamese" while tugging at the eyes. From the perspective of a child, it was a silly little playground song. I had to explain its true meaning and why it was hurtful, even if they and their friends did not mean anything by it.

I have come to realize that being American is not about being White. There are many people of different origins and colors who are part of the American experience. The more stories that we share from more diverse people, the better we understand. And I am part of that big cultural mosaic that is this country. I don't HAVE to or WANT to change my outward appearance to belong.

I look in the mirror now and what do I see? *[Looks in mirror.]* Glasses, same round face, same nose and eyes, a few age spots, I hope a better hairstyle. I see someone who is proud of who she is, where she came from, and what she has learned. Also someone who is lucky that her family survived physical threats at the beginning of her life. I have only known micro aggressions because of my race which never manifested into actual violence against me personally.

Many Black and Asian people cannot say the same thing. Even now. Especially now.

I also see someone who is proud to be both Asian and American.

END OF PLAY

8

DEATH AND THE MATRON

BY DEV LUTHRA

DESCRIPTION:
The seed image of this play is from Lauren Markham's book "A Map of Future Ruins". The play's frame is the story of Savitri impressing Death, from the Mahabharatha.

CHARACTERS:
WOMAN – She wears jeans and a patched long-sleeved top, distressed by months in the jungle

GHOST OF DAUGHTER – 12 or so

DEATH – He has a satchel

ABOUT THE PLAYWRIGHT

Dev Luthra is a theatre maker of South Asian and European descent, trained at East 15 Acting School, London and at Shakespeare & Company, Lenox MA. His plays include Macbeth's Children (co-written with Michael Bettencourt, AATE New Play Award) focusing on the fate of the children in Shakespeare's play and Malcolm's decision to return to a country in the throes of civil war. *Second Chances* focuses on the issues of housing justice as engaged with by an architect and his Thanksgiving dinner guest, a local homeless man. His one act play *Secret Asian Man* focuses on his experience being raised in two cultures. From 2007 to 2022 he served as Artistic Director of And Still We Rise Productions, a theater company committed to the advocacy of the rights of people impacted by the US prison system. Dev has lived and worked in the Northeast since 1978.

(Lights up on the woman. She is squatting, picking out the edible bits from plants scattered about the space. Out of her grunts and chewing noises, a song makes itself. A chant perhaps. Bits from child memories of her daughter, and bits she is making up. She sings as if she is telling herself something. She is making a doll out the bits of plant.)

(The GHOST DAUGHTER enters.)

GHOST DAUGHTER: Don't you miss me?

(WOMAN is stock still for a moment)

WOMAN: You dare ask me?! Of course I miss you. Like a lopped off, lost limb. I feel the ghost of you. I am willing to die here, so you can live there, in the far-off, in that land we dreamt of.

GHOST DAUGHTER: I dream of you every night. I die every time I remember you left me, you gave up and left me in the hands of strangers, straggling strangers. I am in the land of milk and honey: sour milk and bitter honey.

WOMAN: Hush. Don't speak badly of our dream.

GHOST DAUGHTER: Your dream, not mine. Your dream is a lie. It's lying to you still as you rot in this jungle place. Alone. Without me. Without anyone.

WOMAN: Shut your mouth! How dare you! What do you know? You were 11 when I gave you up. Sent you on your way. I could have kept you here with me.

WOMAN (cont'd): But no, I sent you on, because I still believed in some dream future for us, for you. The dream almost killed me. So I starved it. Slowly and surely, I starved it so I could stay here.

GHOST DAUGHTER: You want me to feel sorry for you? I can't believe it! I am the one in the big North. Surrounded by poison and gold. I carry your dream with me now. The dream you dropped, you starved, you abandoned. And you abandoned me!

WOMAN: For a moment. Just for a moment. You disappeared.

> *(They reach toward each other, as if across a chasm. After a beat, GHOST DAUGHTER climbs up and into the north. Stage fades to black.)*
>
> *(DEATH enters. Looks over the audience. Lifts a hand in greeting. Curious, leaning forward, taking time to see who is there. After a while, Death exits. Slowly. Perhaps looks back before disappearing.)*
>
> *(WOMAN sings again. She stutters to a halt just as DEATH re-enters (from a different direction than the exit))*

DEATH: Don't stop now.

WOMAN: …

DEATH: Don't stop. I came all the way here to hear you.

WOMAN: No you didn't.

DEATH: Yes. I did.

WOMAN: I made good money once. I made good money. I kept it and spent it. I made good money once.

DEATH: Sing. Sing for me. Sing. (*pause*) Please.

(WOMAN sings and DEATH dances.)

WOMAN: Why are you here? What do you want?

DEATH: I am here to gather you, reap you like ripe grain.

WOMAN: Am I maize, rye, spelt?

DEATH: You are oats, barley, malt.

WOMAN: Porridge and whiskey. Where will you take me?

DEATH: I will take you – all of you – to the well.

WOMAN: Of course, I should have known. I will drink at the well.

DEATH: Stand up. Come.

(They walk through the jungle. WOMAN has the doll with her. The trees open up to them. There are sounds of wind and birds. They arrive at the well.)

(DEATH stops and turns toward the woman. She puts a pair of sunglasses on him, and another pair on her. The light intensifies.)

DEATH (cont'd):
You are at an end
There is no way forward
There is no way back
You are at an end
Shut your ears to the world
Roll your eyes into the back of
Your mind
You are at an end.

> *(DEATH gestures to seize her, but she shrugs DEATH off. WOMAN and DEATH circling each other. DEATH has a pebbled net in one hand and grabs the doll from WOMAN with the other. WOMAN draws out a pair of Ginzu knives. DEATH is trying to trap WOMAN in the net. Tries to throw WOMAN off guard with the doll.)*

DEATH: Don't make this hard on yourself. Relax. It's time.
(Throws the net.)

WOMAN: Stay back. Stay back I said. *(W tries and fails to gut the net.)*

DEATH: Come on now. Come on. You move well.

WOMAN: Leave me be.

DEATH: Look here. *(Presenting doll. Hypnotizing her.)* Relax. You work so hard. Let me take care of things.

> *(WOMAN falls to her knees. Eyes flitter and close. She forces herself awake with a start. Springs up.)*

DEATH: Stay down. Get back down.

WOMAN: Leave. Me. Be. *She is tiring.*

DEATH: I'm here to take care of you. Take you away from here.

WOMAN: Shut up. You know nothing of me. I chose this place. It is choosing me.

DEATH: What do you mean, choosing you? You like to be chosen? Are you the chosen one? Are you? Well, I choose you. I choose you now. Out of all the people in the world I choose you, to harvest you, to reap you like ripe grain. Yes. Like ripe grain. You belong with me. At the well. With me.

> *(The woman is tempted. She is lonely. DEATH has a warm voice, a clear voice, a comforting voice.)*

Come. Sit. Sit here with me. Rest before we go.

WOMAN: How kind. How considerate. Listen. I am alone in this place. Everyone else is passing through. They are passing through here, chasing something, leaving storms and mudflats, broken walls, doorless rooms behind, leaving children and enemies behind. They are chasing a horizon - something: the wants that won't let them go: a bed and ice and a school day and uncracked doors, a safe place to eat. I gave up all that.

DEATH: You gave up. That's why I am here. To help you give up. You can give up with me. Give it up to me. Forever. Rest forever. *Whispers.* Disappear forever.

WOMAN: Into the well.

DEATH: Yes. The well.

WOMAN: Well, well, well. *(She sings Well, well, well.)*

(DEATH approaches her, drapes the pebbled net over WOMAN's shoulders. She straightens up like a farmer, feet planted. Looks DEATH in the eye.)

WOMAN: I am here to stay.

(WOMAN takes out a knife. Deliberately, she slits death's robe into tatters as he speaks.)

DEATH: You are muscling in on my gig, man.
As soon as I get a bead on someone
They're popped off:
Infected, dejected, rejected, divested
Fleeced, in pieces, mind and body melted
Down into a glowing puddle of
Radio-active waste
I am tired of it.
I was a north star
All looked up to me
All knew they were daily approaching nearer to me
Closer to me
But no longer.
What am I supposed to do now?
I am at a loose end. Pre-empted, tempted
Into lying back and letting you all pour over the cliff
A long remorseless fall into – into – balloon-blobs of
Mist. Fall! Fall woman! Fall! Into the well.

(WOMAN and DEATH wrestle. DEATH falls into the well. Beat. Woman cloaks herself in the pebble net; she settles down on the ground. Singing she refashions a new doll. She places doll somewhere above her. Perhaps places it in the house.)

WOMAN: So carefully
I gave in I allowed myself the
Soft and thrilling sensation
Of possible peace and comfort
Of a future with us in it
Not dead, maimed or lost
But grooved into a routine
Of love and habits, pleasures and
Small problems
No more big problems
And my body collapses
And then my spirit dissolves
And spreads out like water over dry sand
A calm and silent resolve
To stay
To stay alone
Alone without anyone
Pulling me into love and need
Only me
And the trees, the birds, the wind
Will you know me when you see me?
Am I a complete stranger to you?
Is there any part of you that envies me?
Envies me.
Do you envy me my ghost limb of a daughter?
My defeat of death
My alone-ness.
Ply me with glances, stares, questions, judgment.
Sometimes I almost know myself.

(WOMAN takes up doll and cradles it. She buries it. She sings.)

WOMAN: My daughter is underground. Unfound. Unsound. Underground.

END OF PLAY

9

LETTING GO

BY ROSANNA YAMAGIWA ALFARO

CHARACTERS:

ELLEN – mid-20's

HARRIET – her grandmother, late 70's

PLACE: A living room/kitchen with a large picture window. A kitchen table and two chairs stage right; a chair and a TV, stage left.

(Note: a *(/)* indicates a short pause.)

ABOUT THE PLAYWRIGHT

Rosanna Yamagiwa Alfaro has been produced at the Huntington, Pan Asian Repertory, East West Players, and the Magic Theater. She is a former Huntington Playwriting Fellow and MCC Artist Fellow in Playwriting. In early 2024 her "Don't Fence Me In" (dir. Michelle Aguillon) was part of "The Dragonfly Plays" by the Asian American Playwright Collective and the Burlington Players with plays by Hortense Gerardo and Dev Luthra. Her "Tryst" (dir. Daniel Gidron) was produced by the Boston Theater Marathon.

(ELLEN and HARRIET are playing checkers at the kitchen table. ELLEN is dressed in jeans and casual top; HARRIET is wearing an old dress that is missing a few buttons.)

ELLEN: *(to audience)* At 9 a.m. on the day of the open house Grandma and I were playing a game of checkers the way I remember doing when I was little.

HARRIET: So, how many nasty people are coming?

ELLEN: Twenty, maybe thirty. But not to worry. The open house doesn't start until ten. Just keep your mind on the game, O.K.?

HARRIET: Right. Watch me. *(She jumps three men.)* One. Two. Three. You see? One moment's thought, and your old Grandma evens the score.

ELLEN: You cheated!

HARRIET: *(She stands up.)* I won, and now we can have breakfast.

ELLEN: Grandma...

HARRIET: *(She is radiant with expectation.)* Breakfast!

ELLEN: We ate... remember? We had breakfast thirty minutes ago.

HARRIET: *(She is confused.)* Thirty minutes ago.

ELLEN: We had toast with orange marmalade.

HARRIET: With strawberry jam.

ELLEN: You're right. My memory's not so sharp either.

HARRIET: *(She smiles.)* Not so sharp.

ELLEN: Are you hungry?

HARRIET: No. *(She waves the subject away with her hands.)* No.

ELLEN: Shall we play another game of checkers? *(Harriet says nothing.)* What about a cup of coffee?

(HARRIET starts to exit.)

ELLEN (cont'd): I'd like some myself. *(She stands up.)* They say it's good to have the smell of freshly brewed coffee in the air when you're selling a house. It eliminates kitchen odors.

HARRIET: I don't want any coffee.

(She exits to the living room.)

ELLEN: *(to audience)* That was really something, wasn't it? Before I arrived Grandma was probably having a dozen breakfasts a day... She was probably a lot happier than she is now.

(The news blares on the TV. HARRIET tries unsuccessfully to turn it off, switching from channel to channel.)

ELLEN: *(to audience)* At 11:00 Grandma was having problems with the TV.

(HARRIET turns up the volume. ELLEN rushes into the living room.)

ELLEN: Grandma! *(She seizes the remote and turns down the volume.)* Wow, you really had that on full blast. If anyone comes to see the house they won't be able to hear themselves think. You want to change channels? *(Harriet shakes her head.)* You want it off? *(Harriet nods.)* There. That's better.

HARRIET: Better.

ELLEN: You just click this red button. *(She demonstrates. Harriet looks on with interest. Her eyes widen.)* Do you want me to get you something? A book? *(Harriet shakes her head.)* Mom just called from Berkeley and said to post open house signs on all the telephone poles... easy for her to say.

HARRIET: *(She smiles.)* Easy.

ELLEN: Do you want something, something to do?

HARRIET: (/)) I like walking from here to there... and back to here. *(She illustrates and smiles.)*

ELLEN: *(She smiles too.)* Well, that's nice. That's great. *(to audience)* Exercise - that's good for you.

(HARRIET is finishing up her lunch as ELLEN discretely watches her.)

ELLEN: *(to audience)* 12 noon and Grandma was slowly finishing up her lunch.

(to Harriet) I can't believe it. No one's coming to the open house. Mom keeps barking orders from California, but obviously no one's buying houses right now in New Hampshire. We've got to be back in Berkeley by the beginning of September. That's when I start teaching my yoga classes. I told Mom we should rent the house, not sell it.

HARRIET: Sell it. Sell it. *(Her hand shakes as she eats, and her fork clinks against the side of the dish. She has difficulty bringing the food to her mouth.)*

ELLEN: You don't want to feel it's still yours? The grape arbor Mom loved as a child, the bamboo hedge...

HARRIET: Sell it.

ELLEN: You don't think you'll miss it? You'll miss your friends.

HARRIET: No. *(She lowers her head to the rim of the plate.)*

ELLEN: Louise is very nice.

HARRIET: Louise? *(She decides to lift the plate to her mouth and shovel in the last grains of rice.)*

ELLEN: You know. Louise, your next door neighbor. The one who took you to the grocery store every week before I came. She's very nice.

HARRIET: Oh, Louise. *(She smiles and puts down the plate.)* She's not really that nice. *(She picks up her teacup and takes several gulps in quick succession.)*

ELLEN: Grandma, you'll burn yourself.

(HARRIET takes several more gulps, finishing the tea before she lowers the cup.)

ELLEN (cont'd):
(She's not being mean, just concerned and pedagogical.) That tea is boiling hot, Grandma. You realize what you're doing? You're pouring boiling liquid down your throat. *(HARRIET smiles.)* It's as if I took a cup of boiling water and poured it on my hand.

(HARRIET takes another gulp.)

ELLEN: It burns your throat just as it would my hand.

(HARRIET is doing her walk from here to there and back to here.)

ELLEN: *(to audience)* At 2 o'clock since no one had come to the open house I decided to do the wash. (/) Mom made a big mistake. I should have stayed home in Berkeley fixing up the annex, and she should have been here dealing with the move. After all, Mom lived in this house until college. She's the one who knows the town, the people.

(HARRIET crashes into ELLEN.)

ELLEN (cont'd): Careful! (/) Sorry. Are you all right? *(HARRIET smiles.)* I'm going to do the wash. Do you want me to wash anything of yours?

HARRIET: Wash anything of yours?

ELLEN: In the basement. You know. You have a washer and dryer in the basement. *(HARRIET'S eyes widen.)* Maybe I could do your pajamas.

HARRIET: No... no.

ELLEN: Better yet, maybe I could buy you some new pajamas and a new dress. *(She touches Harriet's dress.)* These buttons are coming off.

HARRIET: Buttons.

ELLEN: *(She smiles.)* It's time you spent some money on yourself. You're a rich woman, and Eileen Fisher is having a big sale. I could buy you a new dress and a pair of pajamas for half price.

HARRIET: I want to be... myself.

ELLEN: *(She's struck by this but still persists.)* Look, it can't hurt... yourself... to buy yourself some new clothes.

HARRIET: I'm going to die soon.

ELLEN: That's silly. You should look after yourself, wear something other than old pajamas or one favorite dress. You don't even need to buy a new dress if you don't want to. Your closets are full of dresses. (/) This one is very nice. It's just that you wear it every day.

HARRIET: I don't like your shirt. *(She smiles, touching Ellen's sleeve.)*

ELLEN: What? This is the one you always liked. You told me just yesterday, remember?

HARRIET: *(touching her own dress)* I like my dress.

> *(ELLEN brings a large potted plant into the room and sets it down as HARRIET watches.)*

ELLEN: *(to audience)* It's 5 o'clock and finally a knock at the door. One customer at the end of the day. He didn't want the house, but he liked the plant. *(to Harriet)* He gave me $20 for it.

HARRIET: I don't want his $20.

ELLEN: We can't take it all the way across the country. The man's waiting outside by his car.

> *(HARRIET stops ELLEN as she's about to exit with the plant.)*

ELLEN: What is it, Grandma?

HARRIET: The pot. *(She touches the ceramic pot.)*

ELLEN: You've got so many nice pots. Are you sure you need this one? There're two more just like it in the basement.

HARRIET: I want it.

ELLEN: You want me to rip out the plant.

HARRIET: Rip it out.

ELLEN: No one wants a plant without its pot.

HARRIET: Rip it out.

(As ELLEN speaks HARRIET climbs up on a chair, then onto the kitchen table.)

ELLEN: *(to audience)* It's late afternoon. I took a walk around the neighborhood to take down the open house signs. I knew Grandma hated wasting electricity, but before I left I turned on the kitchen light just in case it started getting dark before I returned.

Grandma was standing on top of the kitchen table, reaching for the light on the ceiling when I got back. She burned herself.

(HARRIET cries out in pain as ELLEN rushes to the rescue.)

ELLEN: Grandma! *(She throws her arms around Harriet's legs to keep her from falling off the table.)* Grandma, you'll hurt yourself! (/) What on earth were you trying to do? *(She lifts Harriet from the table like a child.)*

HARRIET: I was trying to unscrew the bulb.

ELLEN: You could have electrocuted yourself. Or broken a bone. Do you know how long a bone takes to heal? I might have had to leave for Berkeley without you. Are you listening, Grandma? (*She speaks more gently when Harriet says nothing.*) Grandma, please don't ever try to climb up on anything again, O.K.? (*Harriet says nothing.*) O.K.?

HARRIET: (*She points to the bulb.*) It's still afternoon. The light. The light. You turned it on too soon.

(*ELLEN is practicing yoga poses.*)

ELLEN: It's 9 o'clock and I was trying out some yoga poses to teach my students.

(*HARRIET enters. She is barefoot. She has an open milk carton in her hand, holding it at a tilt so the milk sloshes out at every step. Something catches her eye outside the window. The milk carton drops to the floor.*)

ELLEN: Grandma!

HARRIET: It spilled...

ELLEN: Shit! Shit!

(*HARRIET bends down to pick up the carton but drops it again.*)

ELLEN (cont'd): Let me do that. You shouldn't bend down like that. You could hurt yourself.

(HARRIET begins backing out of the room.)

ELLEN: Grandma, I'm sorry. It's just that everything's gone wrong: The light bulb. The open house. The whole fucking day.

HARRIET: Don't talk like that.

ELLEN: *(She laughs.)* Look, if anyone in the world deserves to curse, it's me. *(She shakes her fist at the heavens.)* Did you hear that up there?

HARRIET: *(She speaks softly.)* I hate myself.

ELLEN: What was that? I didn't hear you. (/) Grandma?

HARRIET: I...hate...myself. I hate myself.

(A month later. HARRIET is at the picture window.)

ELLEN: *(to audience)* In the end we sold the house for only a little less than we thought it was worth. The last night we slept there I thought I heard a strange noise. I went down the hall to Grandma's room and she wasn't there so I went to the living room and there she was, looking at the backyard through the picture window. She looked frail and... very lovely. She stood there a long time, her hands pressed against the glass.

END OF PLAY

APPENDIX A

PLAYWRIGHTS' CONTACT INFORMATION

Please contact the individual playwright to obtain the right to perform their work.

MICHELLE M. AGUILLON
michelle.aguillon@gmail.com

CHRISTINA R CHAN
crosechan@live.com

HORTENSE GERARDO
P.O. Box 15195
Boston, MA 02215
Email: hfgerardo@gmail.com
Website: www.hortensegerardo.com
Twitter (X): @hfgerardo
LinkedIn:
https://www.linkedin.com/in/hortense-gerardo-2b824b6
New Play Exchange:
https://newplayexchange.org/users/261/hortense-gerardo

GREG LAM
greg.lam.writing@gmail.com

JAMIE LIN
mslin93@gmail.com

MICHAEL LIN
michael.tsai.lin@gmail.com

VIVIAN LIU-SOMERS
vliusomers@gmail.com

DEV LUTHRA
devluthra@gmail.com
72 Wyman Street,
Jamaica Plain MA 02130

DAVID VALDES
www.davidvaldeswrites.com
Instagram: @davidvaldeswrites

ROSANNA YAMAGIWA ALFARO
alfaros@comcast.net

NOTES

NOTES

NOTES

NOTES

NOTES

ABOUT THE ASIAN AMERICAN PLAYWRIGHT COLLECTIVE

The Asian American Playwright Collective is an all-volunteer group of playwrights based in the Boston area that have banded together to raise awareness about the breadth and depth of new work by theatre artists who are informed by a complex and multi-layered identity, but who also just happen to be Asian American.

Learn more at:

https://aapcboston.wixsite.com/mysite
https://www.facebook.com/aapcboston/
https://twitter.com/AAPCBoston
https://www.instagram.com/aapcboston/

Made in the USA
Middletown, DE
03 November 2024